BRER TIGER
and the BIG WIND

by William J. Faulkner
illustrated by Roberta Wilson

MORROW JUNIOR BOOKS
NEW YORK

Egg tempera was used for the full-color illustrations.
The text type is 16-point Goudy Old Style.

Text copyright © 1995 by The Estate of William J. Faulkner
Illustrations copyright © 1995 by Roberta Wilson

Printed in Hong Kong by South China Printing Company (1988) Ltd.

1 2 3 4 5 6 7 8 9 10

Library of Congress Cataloging-in-Publication Data
Faulkner, William J.
Brer Tiger and the big wind/by William J. Faulkner; illustrated by Roberta Wilson.
p. cm.
Summary: Clever Brer Rabbit finds a way to teach the greedy Brer Tiger a lesson.
ISBN 0-688-12985-4 (trade)—ISBN 0-688-12986-2 (library)
[1. Afro-Americans—Folklore.   2. Folklore—United States.]   I. Wilson, Roberta, ill.   II. Title.
PZ8.1.F235Br 1995   398.2'089960730452974428—dc20   94-15408   CIP AC

To Frank
—R.W.

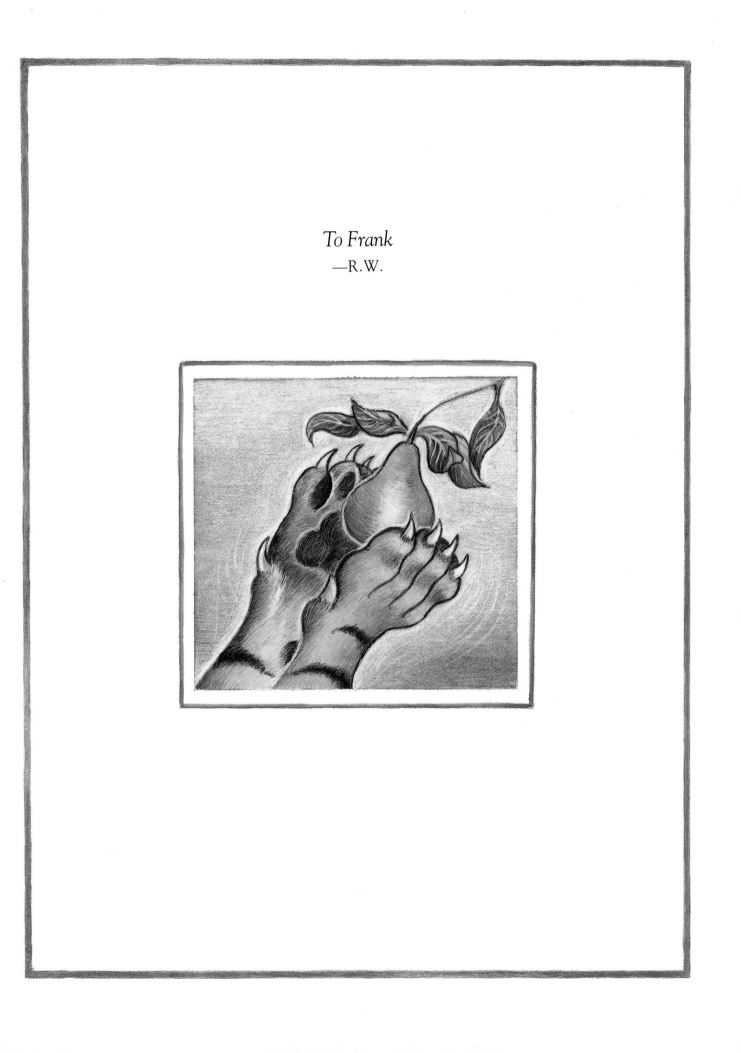

In olden days, the creatures used to plow in the fields and plant their crops the same as menfolks. When the rains came, the crops were good. But one year no rain came, and there was a famine in the land. The sun boiled down like a red ball of fire. All the creeks and ditches and springs dried up. All the fruit on the trees shriveled, and there was no food and no drinking water for the creatures. It was a terrible time.

But there was one place where there was plenty of food and a spring that never ran dry. It was called Clayton Field. And in the field stood a big pear tree, just a-hanging down with juicy pears, enough for everybody.

So the poor hungry creatures went over to the field to get something to eat and something to drink. But a great big Bengal tiger lived under the pear tree, and when the creatures came nigh, he rose up and said, "Wumpf! Wumpf! I'll eat you up. I'll eat you up if you come here!" All the creatures backed off and crawled to the edge of the woods and sat there with misery in their eyes, looking at the field. They were so starved and so parched that their ribs showed through their hides and their tongues hung out of their mouths.

Now, just about that time, along came Brer Rabbit, just a-hopping and a-skipping, as if he'd never been hungry or thirsty in his life.

"Say, what's the matter with you creatures?" asked Brer Rabbit.

"We're hungry and thirsty and can't find any food or water—that's what's the matter with us," answered the creatures. "And we can't get into Clayton Field because Brer Tiger said he'd eat us up if we came over there."

"That's not right," said Brer Rabbit. "It's not right for one animal to have it all and the rest to have nothing. Come here. Come close. I'm going to tell you something." And Brer Rabbit jumped up on a stump so that all could see him as they crowded around. When Brer Rabbit had finished whispering his plan, he said, "Now, you-all be at your posts in the morning; everyone be there before sunup."

The first animal to get to his post was Brer Bear. Before daybreak, he came toting a big club on his shoulder and took his place alongside an old hollow log. The next creature to arrive was Brer Alligator Cooter, a snapping turtle, who crawled in the hollow log. Then Brer Turkey Buzzard and Brer Eagle and all the big fowls of the air came a-sailing in and roosted in the tops of the tall trees. Next to arrive were the tree-climbing animals, like Brer Raccoon and his family and Sis Possum and all her little ones. They climbed into the low trees. Then followed the littler creatures, like Brer Squirrel, Brer Muskrat, Brer Otter, and all kinds of birds. They all took their posts and waited for Brer Rabbit.

Pretty soon, when the sun was about a half hour high, along came Brer Rabbit down the big road with a long grass rope wrapped around his shoulder. And he was just a-singing, "Oh, Lord, oh, Lord, there's a great big wind that's a-coming through the woods, and it's going to blow *all* the people off the earth!" And while he was singing his song, a powerful noise broke out in the woods.

There was Brer Bear a-beating on the hollow log with all his might, *bic-a-bam, bic-a-bam, bic-a-bam, bam, bam!* Inside the log Brer Cooter was a-jumping, *bic-a-boom, bic-a-boom, bic-a-boom, boom, boom.* Brer Turkey Buzzard, Brer Eagle, and Brer Chicken Hawk were a-flapping their wings and a-shaking the big trees, and the trees were a-bending, and the leaves were a-flying. Brer Raccoon and Sis Possum were stirring up a fuss in the low trees, while the littler creatures were a-shaking all the bushes. And on the ground and amongst the leaves the teeny-weeny creatures were a-scrambling around. All in all it sounded like a cyclone was a-coming through the woods!

All this racket so early in the morning woke Brer Tiger out of a deep sleep, and he rushed to the big road to see what was going on. "What's going on out there, huh?" he growled. "What's going on out there?"

All of the creatures were too scared to say anything to Brer Tiger. They just looked at him and hollered for Brer Rabbit to "Tie me! Please, sir, tie me!"

Now, all this time Brer Rabbit just kept a-hollering, "There's a *great* big cyclone a-coming through the woods that's going to *blow* all the people off the earth!" And the animals just kept a-making their noise and a-hollering, "Tie me, Brer Rabbit. Tie me."

When Brer Rabbit came around by Brer Tiger, Brer Tiger roared out, "Brer Rabbit, I want you to tie me. I don't want the big wind to blow *me* off the earth!"

"I don't have time to tie you, Brer Tiger. I've got to go down the road to tie those other folks to keep the wind from blowing *them* off the earth. Because it sure looks to me like a *great big hurricane* is a-coming through these woods."

Brer Tiger looked toward the woods, where Brer Bear was a-beating and Brer Cooter was a-jumping and the birds were a-flapping and the trees were a-bending and the leaves were a-flying and the bushes were a-shaking and the wind was a-blowing, and it seemed to him as if Judgment Day had come.

Old Brer Tiger was so scared he couldn't move. And then he said to Brer Rabbit, "Look-a-here, I've got my head up against this pine tree. It won't take but a minute to tie me to it. Please tie me, Brer Rabbit. Tie me, because I don't want the wind to blow me off the face of the earth."

Brer Rabbit shook his head. "Brer Tiger, I don't have time to bother with you. I have to go tie those other folks; I told you."

"I don't care about those other folks," said Brer Tiger. "I want you to tie *me* so the wind won't blow *me* off the earth. Look, Brer Rabbit, I've got my head here against this tree. Please, sir, tie me."

"All right, Brer Tiger. Just hold still a minute, and I'll take out time to save your striped hide," said Brer Rabbit.

Now, while all this talking was going on, the noise kept getting louder and louder. Somewhere back yonder it sounded like thunder was a-rolling! Brer Bear was still a-beating on the log, *bic-a-bam, bic-a-bam, bic-a-bam, bam, bam!* Brer Cooter was still a-jumping in the log, *bic-a-boom, bic-a-boom, bic-a-boom, boom, boom!* And the birds were a-flapping and the trees were a-bending and the leaves were a-flying and the bushes were a-shaking and the creatures were a-crying—and Brer Rabbit was a-tying!

He wrapped the rope around Brer Tiger's neck, and he pulled it
tight; he wrapped it around Brer Tiger's feet, and he pulled it tight.
Then Brer Tiger tried to pitch and rear, and he asked Brer Rabbit to
tie him a little tighter, "because I don't want the big wind to blow
me off the earth." So Brer Rabbit wrapped him around and around
so tight that even the biggest cyclone in the world couldn't blow
him away. And then Brer Rabbit backed off and looked at Brer
Tiger.

When he saw that Brer Tiger couldn't move, Brer Rabbit called out, "Hush your fuss, children. Stop all of your crying. Come down here. I want to show you something. Look, there's our great Brer Tiger. He had all the pears and all the drinking water and all of everything, enough for everybody. But he wouldn't give a bite of food or a drop of water to anybody, no matter how much they needed it. So now, Brer Tiger, you just stay there until those ropes drop off you. And you, children, gather up your crocus sacks and water buckets. Get all the pears and drinking water you want, because the Good Lord doesn't love a stingy man. He put the food and water here for all His creatures to enjoy."

After the animals had filled their sacks and buckets, they all joined in a song of thanks to the Lord for their leader, Brer Rabbit, who had shown them how to work together to defeat their enemy, Brer Tiger.

ABOUT THE AUTHOR

William J. Faulkner (1891–1987) grew up on his widowed mother's farm in Society Hill, South Carolina. When Simon Brown, a gifted storyteller and former slave, came to work on the farm, young Faulkner was riveted by his tales of slave life and of animals that talked, among them "Brer Tiger and the Big Wind." Faulkner was inspired to become a folklorist and storyteller himself, and throughout his life he remembered and retold Simon Brown's tales.

Faulkner wrote:

> The Afro-American slaves had no weapons against their oppressors. So, like their forebears in Africa, they used their folklore to comment on good and evil in their lives, depending on the cloak of fiction to protect themselves and their families from retribution. Many of the animal stories of black Americans were clever denunciations of the brutal slave system.

Faulkner received his doctorate in theology from the Chicago Theological Seminary. He held a variety of posts, including that of pastor of churches in Chicago and Atlanta and university minister and dean of men at Fisk University in Nashville. Until well into his eighties he traveled throughout the country, telling stories and speaking about folklore to children, college students, and adults.